THIS CANDLEWICK BOOK BELONGS TO:

_____

_____

_____

_____

To Ka-Tai Lau with thanks,
T.H.

The author and publishers wish to thank
Martin Jenkins for his invaluable
assistance in the preparation of this book.

Text copyright © 1992 by Judy Allen
Illustrations copyright © 1992 by Tudor Humphries

First U.S. paperback edition 1994
First published in Great Britain in 1992 by Walker Books Ltd., London.

Library of Congress Cataloging-in-Publication Data.

Allen, Judy.
Tiger / Judy Allen ; illustrated by Tudor Humphries.
Summary: When the villagers hire a famous hunter to kill the tiger rumored to live in the woods, only one
young boy wishes to protect the animal; and, in fact, the hunter knows more than one way to shoot a tiger.
ISBN 1-56402-083-5 (hardcover)
[1. Tigers—Fiction. 2. China—Fiction.] I. Humphries, Tudor, ill. II. Title.
PZ7.A4237Ti   1992
[E]—dc20   91-58760
ISBN 1-56402-284-6 (paperback)

10 9 8 7 6 5 4 3 2 1

Printed in Hong Kong

The pictures for this book were done in watercolor.

Candlewick Press
2067 Massachusetts Avenue
Cambridge, Massachusetts 02140

TIGER

by
Judy Allen

illustrated by
Tudor Humphries

CANDLEWICK PRESS
CAMBRIDGE, MASSACHUSETTS

"There is a tiger," the villagers told each other.
"Out beyond the rice fields, out beyond the
swamp, somewhere in the oak woods near
the river bank, there is a tiger."

No one was sure where the rumor had started, but it was a strong one, and most people believed it. They began to discuss the best, and safest, way to kill the tiger.

"But why kill it?" said Lee, who was the youngest of the children if you didn't count the babies. "Because if you eat the meat of a tiger," said his uncle, "you yourself become as brave as the tiger. Which is why it's a bad idea to poison it."

"Also, its skin can be sold for an enormous amount of money," said his father. "Which is why it's a bad idea to set metal traps. They might damage it and lower the value."

"Lee," said his uncle, "you must never tell anyone outside the village what we're planning. It's against the law to sell a tiger skin, and we could go to jail."

"I'll never tell," said Lee.

Later, he asked his mother if eating tiger meat really made you brave.

"You're as brave as you think you are," said his mother. "Eating a rose petal will make you brave—if you believe it will."

Lee looked out over the fields toward the swamp and the oak woods beyond.

"I don't want them to kill it," he said.

"It's probably just a story," said his mother. "It probably isn't there at all."

"It is there," said Lee. "I know it is."

A few days after the tiger rumor, another rumor started. The new one was about a great hunter who traveled vast distances looking for exciting prey. This was also a strong rumor. Everyone who passed it on knew someone, who knew someone else, who had heard from a reliable witness that this hunter had never once failed. Also, he was traveling in the direction of the village.

"That's handy," said Lee's uncle.

"We'll have to pay him," objected Lee's father.

"Better to get the tiger and give away some of the profit than to go after it ourselves and fail—or be killed," said Lee's uncle.

Not long after the rumor, the hunter himself arrived. He ate the food they offered. He listened while they told him about the magical meat and the money to be made from the skin, and then he got ready to begin. Several men offered to go with him to help dig a pit for the tiger to fall into or to carry the carcass home, but he refused them.

"To find the tiger," he said, "I need to travel quietly and alone. If I need you later, I'll send for you."

"Good hunting," said the villagers—all but one.

"Bad hunting," said Lee. "I hope it gets away."

The hunter stared at Lee.

Lee stood straight and stared back.

The hunter turned and walked out of the village. "How will he kill it?" whispered Lee's uncle as he went.

"Shoot it," said Lee's father. "I think I saw a gun in his pack with a telephoto lens, so he doesn't have to get too close."

By early evening the hunter was walking slowly by
the edge of the oak woods, near the river. Sometimes
he crouched down and looked at the ground. Every now
and then, as he crouched and looked, he saw the footprints
of a large animal in the damp earth of the riverbank.
"Pug marks," said the hunter to himself, moving ever
more slowly, ever more quietly.
After a time he came to a clearing. An animal lay in the
clearing, a deer. It was dead and had been partly eaten.
The hunter sat down beside a tangled bush and waited.
Behind him a tree rustled. There was a sound like a rug
being shaken in the wind, and then a huge bird flopped
down onto the deer and stabbed at it with its beak.
Another followed.

But before the second vulture could start to eat,
something burst out of the long grass at the edge of the
trees and ran at the birds. It was a big golden cat with dark
markings that were so like the shadows of branches and
grass stems, that it had been invisible until it moved.
"Tiger," whispered the hunter to himself.
The first vulture flapped clumsily into the air. The
tiger cuffed the second, slower bird with its great paw.
Then it got a firm grip on its prey with its jaws and
dragged it steadily, quickly, back under the shelter of the
oak where it had been dozing.
"A fine male," said the hunter to himself. "Fully grown,
but young."
The tiger began to eat the rest of the meat.
"I must try to get a shot from here," thought the hunter,
"but the angle is difficult and the tree is in the way.
I need to be an arm's length to the right."

He moved very cautiously, very gently, but the tiger's sharp ears caught the sound. It raised its head, showed its teeth in a silent snarl—and was gone.

"That was a foolish mistake," thought the hunter.

"I must be more careful."

He waited through the night. At dawn he sought out the fresh trail and began to follow it.

It was two days before he saw the tiger again. It was some distance from him, walking around a craggy outcrop below a small cliff.

He watched it sniffing at a huge rock in a particular way.

"There is a female somewhere around," said the hunter to himself. "You'll find her when she's ready."

The tiger moved on, behind the rock and out of sight. The hunter followed silently.

By the light of the evening sun, he watched it sharpening its claws on the bark of a tree, stretching its full length against the trunk. He got it in his sights, but at the last second, even though it didn't hear him, didn't see him, the tiger moved and spoiled his shot.

At dusk he watched it washing its golden striped fur with great sweeps of its rough tongue.

"I can't take you now," thought the hunter. "The light is bad, and the shadows make it hard to judge the distance." That night he watched it stalk another deer, creeping so slowly through the undergrowth that sometimes it didn't seem to move at all for almost ten minutes.

"You are as patient as I am," thought the hunter.

He watched it make its leap. He watched the deer spring away and the tiger go for its hindquarters and miss. The deer ran. The tiger didn't chase it. All its power had gone into the first attack.

"You probably always miss more than you catch," the hunter thought. "But it doesn't matter. You're sleek and well fed."

The next day, in the heat of the afternoon, he watched the tiger drink from the river, and then fling itself into the water with a great splash, and swim strongly downstream, just for the cool pleasure of it.

That was when he got his first clear shot, as the water streamed off the tiger's head, and its body undulated just below the surface.

The tiger saw him. It clambered out of the water and shook like a dog, sending drops sparkling all around.

That was when the hunter got his second shot.

The tiger faced him.

"You're no man-eater," said the Hunter. "You with your sharp teeth and strong bones—you live on wild deer and wild pig. You won't go for me."

And he got the fine head and great chest right in his sights and took the third shot.

The tiger snarled to warn him not to come any closer,
but it did not attempt to attack him. It turned its back,
as if with scorn, and loped elegantly away and out of
sight, in among the oak trees.
The hunter packed away his camera and rested for a while
before beginning the trek back to the village.

When he returned, the villagers hurried to meet him.

"Do you need us now, to carry him?" said Lee's father.

"I'm sorry," said the hunter, "not to bring the news you want, but I'm afraid there's nothing to carry."

"But there is a tiger out there?" said Lee's uncle.

"I am the best tracker and the best hunter in the region," said the hunter. "I have covered the whole area you spoke of. If there was a tiger, I would have seen him."

"Do you mean you *didn't* see a tiger?" said Lee's uncle.

The hunter stared at him. Lee's uncle began to fidget.

"Are you trying to pick a fight with me?" said the hunter.

"No," said Lee's uncle quickly, remembering that he had never eaten tiger meat in his life.

"You're very wise," said the hunter, who had never eaten it either. "I'll be on my way, then."

"So it was only a rumor," sighed the villagers, and they shrugged off their disappointment and returned to work.

As the hunter passed by, Lee stepped out in front of him.

"There is a tiger, isn't there?" he said. "I know there is—but I'll never tell."

The hunter stared down at him. Then he smiled.

Then he winked. Then he continued on his way.

Out in the grassy clearing, beyond the rice fields, beyond the swamp, behind the oak woods, the tiger rested on his back in the shade, one fat paw drooping comfortably onto his white chest.

TIGER FACT SHEET

Only a hundred years ago, tigers were found in most parts of Asia, from Turkey all the way to Siberia and Manchuria. They have now disappeared from many parts of this range. The last of the Bali tigers was shot sixty years ago, and the Javan and Caspian tiger have also gone forever. There are between five hundred and one thousand Sumatran tigers left, and about one thousand Siberian tigers, half of these in zoos. The Indo-Chinese tiger is still quite numerous, and the Indian tiger is doing reasonably well. There are at least four thousand of them, and they may even be increasing slowly in number. There are probably fewer than fifty South Chinese tigers – like the one in the story – and it is quite likely that this tiger may become extinct.

WHAT ARE THE DANGERS FOR TIGERS?

People cut down the forests where tigers live to make fields for growing crops and to use the wood from the trees. They hunt tigers because they are afraid of them, and because tigers sometimes prey on their livestock. People also kill tigers for their fur and for their meat and bones, which are used for medicines in the Far East.

IS ANYONE HELPING TIGERS?

Yes. Almost all the governments of countries where tigers live have made it illegal to kill them. They have also set up national parks and reserves where tigers and other wild animals should be able to live undisturbed. There are two organizations which have tried to help governments save their tigers:

The World Wide Fund for Nature
1250 24th St. NW
Washington, DC 20037

IUCN – The International Union for the Conservation of Nature
1400 16th St. NW
Washington, DC 20036

ARE EFFORTS TO SAVE TIGERS SUCCEEDING?

In some places. Project Tiger, started in India in 1973, has helped to increase the number of tigers in India, but in most other places tigers are still decreasing because poachers still hunt them, and there are not enough reserves to protect them.

IS THERE ANYTHING YOU CAN DO?

Yes. You can join the junior section of the World Wide Fund for Nature, or persuade your family or your school to join.

JUDY ALLEN worked in a literary agency and as a book editor before turning to free-lance writing. Her first book — a novel for children — was published in 1973. Since then she has written many books for children, including *Panda, Whale, Elephant,* and *Seal,* each story dramatizing the plight of an endangered species.

TUDOR HUMPHRIES spent most of his childhood engrossed in ancient history, mythology, and nonstop drawing. He has always enjoyed and been involved with children, taking part in children's art festivals and teaching art in primary schools. He has illustrated each of the books in Judy Allen's endangered animals series.